MATT AND DAVE

YUCK'S
ADVE

YUCK'S
DOG

Illustrated by Nigel Baines

www.yuckweb.com

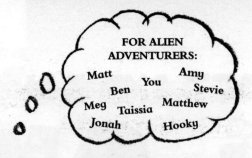

FOR ALIEN
ADVENTURERS:

Matt   Amy

Ben   You   Stevie

Meg   Taissia   Matthew

Jonah   Hooky

SIMON AND SCHUSTER

First published in Great Britain in 2008
by Simon & Schuster UK Ltd
A CBS COMPANY

Africa House 64–78 Kingsway London WC2B 6AH

1 3 5 7 9 10 8 6 4 2

A CIP catalogue record for this book is
available from the British Library

ISBN 978-1-8473-8285-6

Printed and bound in Great Britain by
Cox & Wyman Ltd Reading Berkshire

www.simonsays.co.uk
www.yuckweb.com

There was a boy so disgusting they called him Yuck

YUCK'S ALIEN ADVENTURE

Yuck pressed the FIRE button on the controller as fast as he could...

POW!
BLAST!
ZAP!

He was playing ALIEN RAIDERS. He was Captain Alien on a mission to invade Planet Earth. ALIEN RAIDERS was the greatest computer game ever!

Yuck blasted and zapped, shrinking the enemy army with his minimizer ray.

"Yuck, have you done your homework?" Mum called from downstairs.

"Yes, Mum," Yuck replied.

His sister Polly Princess opened the bedroom door. "No you haven't," she said. "All you've done is play that stupid game all weekend."

Polly was holding a bag full of sweets.

Yuck pressed PAUSE. "Where did you get those sweets from?" he asked.

"Mum gave them to me," Polly told him.

Mum came into Yuck's room.

"Mum! Can I have some sweets too?"
Yuck asked.

Mum pulled the plug
from the wall, turning
off ALIEN RAIDERS.
"No you can't," she
said. "You haven't done
your homework."

"You only get sweets for being good,"
Polly said. She licked her lips then stuck her
tongue out at Yuck. It was blue from
sucking a Blueberry Burst.

Mum went downstairs and Polly
followed her, giggling.

Yuck decided that when he was EMPEROR OF EVERYTHING no one would do any homework. It would be the LAW. Instead, everyone would play ALIEN RAIDERS and eat sweets all day long. Polly would be tied to the REVOLTING ROCKET and blasted out of the universe.

The next morning, when Yuck arrived at school, Mrs Wagon the Dragon was standing at the front of the classroom, collecting everyone's homework.

Yuck crept to his desk.

"Not so fast!" the Dragon said, hooking the handle of her umbrella around his neck. She dragged him towards her. "Where's your homework?"

"It's, er…"

The Dragon stared angrily at Yuck. "You haven't done it, have you?"

"It's not my fault, Miss. I tried to do it but I was kidnapped by aliens."

The Dragon whacked Yuck with her umbrella. "Don't lie!" she said.

"I was, Miss. I promise I was. They took me to their planet in a flying saucer and wouldn't let me go."

"Don't be ridiculous! I want your homework first thing tomorrow or I shall be contacting your parents!"

She booted Yuck to the back of the class. He landed in his seat next to Little Eric.

"I got to level five," Yuck whispered.

"Me too," Little Eric said. "ALIEN RAIDERS is brilliant."

From the desk in front, Frank the Tank turned round, chewing a fizzbomb. "You weren't kidnapped by aliens," he said.

"Yes I was. I can prove it!" Yuck told him.

Yuck bent down under his desk and dug his finger up his nose, pulling out a big sticky bogey. Then he pulled out another and then another. He sat up with the big sticky bogeys all over his hand.

"Look!" he said. "Alien gloop!"

"Alien gloop? What's that?" Frank the Tank asked, staring at the green goo. He reached out and touched it.

"It's from outer space," Yuck explained. "It's what aliens are made of."

"Wow!" Frank the Tank said.

"I'll swap it with you," Yuck told him. "Two of your sweets for my alien gloop."

"It's a deal," Frank the Tank said. He gave Yuck two Fizzbombs then unpeeled the big sticky bogeys from Yuck's fingers.

Rockits! Yuck thought, popping a Fizzbomb into his mouth. He gave the other one to Little Eric. "At lunchtime, we'll get lots more sweets," he said.

That lunchtime, Yuck and Little Eric carried a table into the playground.

Fartin Martin and Tom Bum came over. "What are you doing?" they asked.

"Getting sweets," Yuck said. "Come on, help us. We need lots of bogeys."

Yuck wrote a sign on a piece of card saying **ALIEN GLOOP FOR SALE**.

Yuck, Fartin Martin, Tom Bum and Little Eric began picking their noses and wiping their bogeys on the table.

Frank the Tank and Ben Bong came over to take a look.

Frank the Tank was playing with his alien gloop. "Are aliens really made from alien gloop?" he asked.

"Yes," Yuck told him. "They're gooey and green with lots of eyes, and they have minimizer rays that shrink you to the size of a bogey."

Ben Bong looked at the green gloop on the table. "How much does it cost?" he asked.

"You can have the big bits for three sweets, the stringy bits for two sweets and the little crusty bits for one sweet each."

"I'll have a big bit, please," Ben Bong said, handing over two Toffee Tongue Twisters and a Jelly Snake.

Suzy Shoes and Kate the Skate walked over. "What's happening here?" they asked.

"Yuck's selling alien gloop," Ben Bong told them.

"He was kidnapped by aliens," Frank the Tank said.

"But there's no such thing as aliens," Suzy Shoes said.

"Yes there is," Yuck told her. "They took me to their planet."

He pointed to the gloop on the table. "This came all the way from outer space."

16

"Wow!" Kate the Skate said. She handed over two Lemon Dazzlers for a long stringy bit. Suzy Shoes took a small crusty bit in exchange for a Peppermint Twirl.

"Come and get your alien gloop!" Yuck called across the playground.

Soon everyone came over to see. First came Eddy the Egg, then Tall Paul, then Megan the Mouth. People lined up to buy their alien gloop. Before long a queue had formed.

Polly Princess and Juicy Lucy
pushed to the front of the queue.
"What are you doing,
Yuck?" Polly asked, chewing
on a Liquorice Lace.
"Yuck was kidnapped
by aliens," Megan the
Mouth told her.
"From outer space!"
Eddy the Egg said.

"No he wasn't," Polly replied. "Yuck was at home playing computer games all weekend."

"Then how come I've got alien gloop?" Yuck said.

Polly looked at the table.

"Do you want some?" Little Eric asked her, spying Polly's sweets.

"You're not having MY sweets!" Polly said. "I'm telling the Reaper!"

She ran off and returned with Mr Reaper the headmaster. He saw the crowd gathered around the table. "What's going on here?" he demanded.

Yuck, Fartin Martin, Tom Bum and Little Eric stuffed the sweets into their pockets.

"Yuck's selling alien gloop, Sir," Polly told him.

"Everyone go to your classes immediately!" the Reaper ordered.

Everyone walked back into school, playing with their alien gloop.

Yuck and his friends tried to creep away from the table.

"Not you, Yuck," the Reaper called. The headmaster was looking closely at the table, inspecting the sticky green gloop. "This isn't alien gloop. These are bogeys!"

"No they're not, Sir," Yuck said.

The Reaper looked at Yuck's sign: **ALIEN GLOOP FOR SALE**. "Empty your pockets, now!" he ordered.

Yuck, Fartin Martin, Tom Bum and Little Eric turned their pockets inside out and their sweets fell to the ground.

"All these sweets are confiscated!" the Reaper said, picking them up. "Now get to your class!"

Yuck, Fartin Martin, Tom Bum and Little Eric headed into school.

"That's not fair," Tom Bum said. "He's taken our sweets."

"We've got to get them back," Fartin Martin said.

"But how?" Little Eric asked.

"Tomorrow we'll go on an Alien Raid," Yuck told them.

That evening, at home, Yuck prepared for the raid. While Polly was doing her homework, and Mum and Dad were watching television, Yuck went to his bedroom and began gathering bogeys in a large plastic bag. He scraped big crusty bogeys from his bedroom wall, picked fluffy round bogeys from his carpet and peeled long stringy bogeys from under his bed.

He grabbed his bogey jar and pulled out fistfuls of sticky bogeys, throwing them on top, then he blew his nose into his hands and splattered wet bogeys into the bag until it was full.

Then from his wardrobe he took out a tube of Bouncy-ball Eyeballs and four Deep Space walkie-talkies. He laid them by his door, ready for the morning.

"Yuck, it's bedtime. Have you done your homework?" Mum called from downstairs.

"Yes, Mum," Yuck replied.

He smiled. Tomorrow the Alien Raid would begin.

That night, Yuck dreamed that aliens were invading planet Earth. They flew down in flying saucers and hovered over his school, blasting it with sticky green gloop. They zapped their minimizers at the Reaper, shrinking him to the size of a bogey, and Yuck flicked him into outer space.

The next morning, when Yuck arrived at class, the Dragon pinned him to the wall with the tip of her umbrella. "Have you done your homework?" she demanded.

"I tried to, Miss, but I was kidnapped by aliens – AGAIN!"

"Nonsense!" the Dragon said.

"No it's true, Miss. They're here. They're invading planet Earth."

"Don't lie," the Dragon said. "You're in BIG TROUBLE now. I'll be speaking to your parents about this!"

"But, Miss—"

"No buts," she said, giving him a poke.

Yuck ran to the back of the class and sat next to Little Eric. "Did you bring your bogeys?" he whispered.

Little Eric picked up a plastic bag from under his desk. It was full and bulging.

"Brilliant," Yuck said. He looked across the classroom at Fartin Martin and Tom Bum. Under their desks, each had a bulging plastic bag. Yuck gave them the thumbs up.

That lunchtime, Yuck, Fartin Martin, Tom Bum and Little Eric met behind the bushes at the edge of the playground.

It was time for the Alien Raid.

"Everyone get into disguise," Yuck said.

From their bags, they each scooped out handful after handful of bogeys. They smeared the bogeys onto their faces then down their arms and legs, covering themselves until they were gloopy and green all over. Yuck handed out Bouncy-ball Eyeballs and they stuck them to their heads. They looked just like aliens.

"First we'll attack the school. Then, when the Reaper comes out of his office, we'll dash in and grab our sweets."

 He handed everyone a Deep Space walkie-talkie. "We'll need to split up. We'll communicate by codename. I'll be Captain Alien."

"I'll be the Fartinator," Fartin Martin said.

"I'll be Bumageddon," Tom Bum said.

"I'll be Uranus," Little Eric said.

They ran off and got into position.

Yuck crept to the side of the school and hid beneath a classroom window. He spoke into his walkie-talkie. "Captain Alien here. Is everyone ready?"

"The Fartinator's ready," Fartin Martin said. He was hiding up a tree at the side of the playground.

"Bumageddon's ready," Tom Bum said. He was positioned in the toilets.

"Uranus is ready," Little Eric said. He was behind the door of the canteen.

"Let the Alien Raid begin!" Yuck said.

Little Eric went first. He opened the canteen door and threw in handful after handful of sticky bogeys. Inside, everyone was eating their lunch. The bogeys stuck to their heads and splattered their food.

"UURGH!" Tall Paul said, eating a bogey-covered chip.

Little Eric ran in, covered in alien gloop.

"Aaaggghhh! It's an alien!" everyone screamed. They began running outside to escape.

"Fartinator, get ready," Little Eric said into his walkie-talkie.

Fartin Martin was hiding in the tree.

As everyone ran out into the playground, he threw down handful after handful of bogeys.

They splattered the crowd.

"UURRGH!" Spoilt Jessica said, as a bogey landed in her eye.

Fartin Martin jumped down, covered in alien gloop.

"Aaaggghhh! It's an alien!" everyone screamed. They turned and ran indoors, rushing down the corridor.

"Bumageddon, get ready," Fartin Martin said into his walkie-talkie.

Tom Bum peered out from the toilets. He chucked handful after handful of bogeys up and down the corridor.

They splattered the crowd.

"UUURGH!" the Twinkletrout cried, as a big sticky bogey blasted her ear.

Tom Bum ran out from the toilets, covered in alien gloop.

"Aaaggghhh! It's an alien!" everyone screamed, running for cover in their classrooms.

"Captain Alien, get ready," Tom Bum said into his walkie-talkie.

Yuck was outside the window to Miss Fortune's classroom. As everyone raced in, he threw handfuls of bogeys through the window. They splattered the class.

"URRGH!" Juicy Lucy screamed, as a long stringy bogey wrapped around her neck.

Yuck jumped up at the window.

"Aaaggghhh! It's an alien!"

Polly looked. "No it's not. It's Yuck!" she said.

Yuck ran along the side of the school, throwing bogeys into every room.

"We're under attack!" everyone screamed.

The Reaper came out to see what all the fuss was. When Yuck saw him, he ran to the Reaper's office and peered in through the window. The confiscated sweets were in a jar on the Reaper's desk.

"Calling all aliens. Calling all aliens," Yuck said into his walkie-talkie. "Raid successful. Come and get your sweets!"

Yuck climbed in through the office window, and Fartin Martin, Tom Bum and Little Eric ran to join him. They climbed in after him then all dipped their hands into the jar, scoffing the sweets.

Just then, Polly Princess burst through the office door. "Caught you!" she said.

"Go away, Earthling!" Yuck ordered.

Polly pulled the Bouncy-ball Eyeballs from Yuck's face. "I knew it was you, Yuck!"

She grabbed the jar of sweets.

"Hey! Give those back!" Yuck said.

"I'm telling the Reaper!" Polly said, running out with the jar.

"Oh no! What are we going to do now?" Little Eric asked.

Tom Bum and Fartin Martin took off their Bogey-ball Eyeballs and wiped the bogeys from their faces. "We'll have to pretend it wasn't us."

Suddenly, the room filled with a dazzling white light.

Yuck pointed out of the window. "Look!"

In the sky, a bright white object was descending towards the school.

"What is it?" Tom Bum asked.

"It's a flying saucer!" Yuck said.

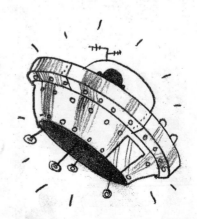

The flying saucer landed outside the Reaper's office. From it, a metal ramp lowered to the ground.

A small green creature stepped out. It had four eyes.

"Wow! It's an alien!" Yuck said.

"A real one!" Tom Bum said.

"What's an alien doing here?" Fartin Martin asked.

The alien walked towards the window. "Greetings, Earthlings. I've come for my sweets."

Yuck stared at the alien in amazement.

It pointed to Yuck's Deep Space walkie-talkie lying on the Reaper's desk. "You called on the communicator," the alien told him. "You said the raid was successful."

"It must have intercepted the signal," Little Eric whispered to Yuck.

"The sweets have gone," Yuck explained to the alien. "My sister stole them."

Yuck could hear Polly and the Reaper marching back along the corridor.

"It wasn't aliens, Sir," Polly was saying. "It was Yuck and his friends. They were after these sweets."

"Quick! We have to get out of here," Yuck said.

"Come with me," the alien told them.

Yuck, Fartin Martin, Tom Bum and Little Eric climbed out of the office window and followed the alien to the flying saucer.

The office door opened and the Reaper came in holding the jar of sweets. "Where are those boys?" he asked.

"They were here a minute ago," Polly said.

The Reaper looked out of the window and saw the flying saucer taking off.

Yuck, Fartin Martin, Tom Bum and Little Eric were waving from inside.

The Reaper watched as they zoomed away in a flash of bright light.

"Oh no!" he said. "They've been kidnapped – by ALIENS!"

Yuck and his friends looked down as they whizzed through the air. They could see the school getting smaller.

"Where are we going?" Yuck asked the alien.

"To my planet," the alien replied. "My name is Puke."

"My name is Yuck," Yuck told him. "And these are my friends, Fartin Martin, Tom Bum and Little Eric."

The alien flicked a switch on the control panel of the flying saucer and it shot up into space.

They zoomed past the moon, then Mars, then Jupiter and Saturn. They flew so fast that the stars flashed by in a blur.

Yuck could see outer space. Ahead of them was a huge green planet. It looked like an enormous bogey.

"That's my planet," Puke said. "I made it."

"You made it?" Yuck asked. "How?"

"Like this," Puke said. The alien picked his nose then opened a hatch in the flying saucer and flicked the bogey into space. He pointed, and a ray of green light zapped from the end of his finger.

"MAXIMIZE!" Puke said.

The green light hit the bogey and the bogey began to grow.

It expanded to the size of a meteor and then as big as a moon.

"Wow!" Yuck said.

Puke pointed again, and a ray of red light zapped from the end of his finger.

"MINIMIZE!" he said.

The huge bogey began to shrink again.

When it was back to bogey size, Puke reached out from the flying saucer, grabbed it and popped it into his mouth. "Yum," he said, chewing.

Then he pulled a lever and the flying saucer dived towards Puke's planet.

They came in to land, and Yuck, Fartin Martin, Tom Bum and Little Eric all stepped out.

Planet Bogey was sticky and gooey. The ground was green like grass but instead it was made of bogeys.

Yuck's feet squelched as he walked.

Puke led them up a green mountain. At its top, it was crusty and hard. They stopped and looked down. Below them was a bogey city full of aliens.

Aliens were zooming around on bogey hoverbikes. They zipped in and out of stringy bogey skyscrapers and crusty bogey shops. Yuck could see a floating bogey palace and a super-speedy bogey train.

"My home," Puke said.

Puke led them down the mountain and into the city. Each alien they met put a finger up its nose and held out a bogey as a friendly greeting.

"It's polite to eat them," Puke explained.

Yuck and his friends ate every single bogey offered. They were delicious!

All afternoon they explored the planet.

They rode the bogey train through the bogey city, zipping over bogey bridges and into bogey tunnels.

In Bogey Park
they played bogey
soccer, kicking
bouncy bogey
balls into stringy
bogey nets.

They slid down bogey hills on bogey
boards and leapt off bogey jumps.

They explored a huge bogey cave that was hairy and crusty like the inside of a nostril.

They took a bogey boat down a bogey river, and went swimming in a bogey sea.

"It's brilliant here!" Little Eric said.
"Much better than school!" they all agreed.

Meanwhile, on Earth, the Reaper had called their parents to school. "I'm afraid I have bad news," he said. "Your children have been kidnapped by aliens."

"We have to get them back," Fartin Martin's mum said.

"Call the police," Tom Bum's dad said.

"Call the army," Yuck's dad said.

"Call the Prime Minister and the Queen and the—"

"Why don't you use this?" Polly said. She was standing beside the Reaper, holding a Deep Space walkie-talkie that she'd found on the Reaper's desk.

"What is it?" Little Eric's mum asked.

The Reaper took it. "It looks like some kind of alien communicator," he said. He spoke into it. "Calling all aliens. This is Mr Reaper of Planet Earth. Come in aliens."

On Planet Bogey, Yuck and his friends were eating bogey sandwiches, sitting on the edge of Puke's flying saucer, looking out into space. From the control panel they heard a beeping sound.

"What's that?" Yuck asked.

Puke was sitting at the control desk in the flying saucer. "It's the communicator," he said, turning a dial. "Someone's calling from Planet Earth."

The communicator crackled. "This is Mr Reaper here."

"What does HE want?" Little Eric whispered.

"Return the Earthlings immediately," the Reaper said.

Yuck had an idea. He spoke into the communicator. "Greetings," he said. "This is Captain Alien. If you want the Earthlings back, you must pay a ransom."

"What ransom?" the Reaper asked.

"Sweets," Yuck said, trying not to giggle. "A whole jar full of sweets, by the end of the day. If not, you'll never see the Earthlings again."

"But their parents are worried about them," the Reaper said.

"Then you'd better get the sweets quickly," Yuck said. He switched off the communicator and everyone laughed.

Back on Earth, the Reaper was in a panic. "We've got to do what the alien says."

He picked up the jar of sweets from his desk. It was almost empty. "We have to fill this up quickly."

"Polly, you've got sweets," Yuck's mum said. "Put them in the jar."

"But that's not fair," Polly said.

"Empty your pockets, Polly!" the Reaper told her. "This is an emergency. We need your sweets."

Up on Planet Bogey, Puke was powering up the flying saucer. "I guess it's time to go home," he said to Yuck and his friends. "Your parents are worried."

Yuck, Fartin Martin, Tom Bum and Little Eric climbed into the flying saucer.

Puke started the thrusters and they took off, flying back through outer space.

They did a quick loop around the Sun then whizzed past the Milky Way back to Planet Earth.

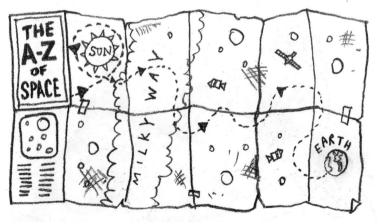

The flying saucer hovered high in the sky, then zoomed down to the school playground. They could see their parents waiting for them.

The flying saucer came in to land. It touched down and the metal ramp lowered. Yuck stepped out.

The Reaper came walking towards him, carrying the jar of sweets.

Yuck took the jar. "I have to give these sweets to the aliens, Sir, or they won't release the others."

Yuck stepped back into the flying saucer.
"Here you are," he said, handing the sweets
to Puke.

"Don't you want any?" Puke asked.

"Will you bring them to us later,
please?" Yuck said. "I have a plan."

Yuck whispered something into Puke's
ear and the alien giggled.

Yuck, Fartin Martin, Tom Bum and Little
Eric stepped out of the flying saucer.

"Hooray! You made it safely!" their
parents cheered.

Yuck's mum gave him a hug. "I'm so
glad you're OK!"

"Let's go home now, Yuck," Dad said.

"Not so fast!" a voice boomed.

The Dragon came running into the playground to speak to Yuck's parents. "Your son is in BIG TROUBLE. He's been telling lies," she said. "He told me he was kidnapped by aliens."

Mum pointed to the flying saucer. It was taking off, zooming up through the sky. "He was telling the truth, Mrs Wagon."

Yuck looked at the Dragon and smiled. "I'd never lie, Miss," he said, giggling.

That evening, at home, Yuck watched
from his bedroom as a bright light flew
down through the dark sky. It was Puke in
his flying saucer.

The flying saucer hovered
above the garden. A hatch
opened and sweets began
falling from it. Yuck saw a
green ray of light.

"MAXIMIZE!" he heard,
as the light zapped the falling sweets.

They fell into the garden with a THUD!

Yuck smiled then ran to Polly's room.
"Polly, I've got something to show you,"
he said.

Polly glared at him. "Go away, Yuck."

"I just thought you might want to share
my sweets," Yuck told her.

"What sweets?"

Yuck walked to her window and opened
the curtains.

Polly stared. On the lawn outside was a
pile of ENORMOUS sweets.

They looked just like HER sweets but they were MUCH BIGGER.

"That's not fair!" she said. "You can't have those!"

Polly ran out of her room and Yuck raced after her. She ran through the kitchen and out into the garden.

"They're MY sweets!" she said, running across the lawn towards a huge strawberry swirl. It was almost as big as Polly.

Yuck looked up. The flying saucer was hovering above the house. He gave the thumbs up and Puke fired a red ray of light, zapping Polly.

"MINIMIZE!" Yuck heard.

"AAAGGGHHH!" Polly cried.

She started shrinking.

"Mum!" she called.

But as she shrank, her voice shrank too. Soon she was as small as a bogey.

Yuck picked her up. "Polly, did you say something?" he asked.

Polly jumped up and down on the palm of his hand.

"I hate you, YUCK!" she squeaked.

As Mum and Dad came running out to
see what was happening, Yuck slipped Polly
into his back pocket.

"What's going on here, Yuck?" Mum
asked. "Where did these enormous sweets
come from?"

"They're my sweets," Yuck said, finishing
a giant marshmallow.

"And where's Polly?" Dad asked.

Yuck swallowed a mouthful of marshmallow then did a big bottom burp. He giggled as a tiny coughing sound came from his back pocket.

"I've got bad news," he said.

He pointed upwards at the flying saucer soaring away into the night sky.

"Polly's been kidnapped by aliens!"

YUCK'S SLOBBERY DOG

Yuck was walking home from school with his sister Polly Princess. She was clutching a Chocolog chocolate bar.

"Where did you get that?" Yuck asked.

"Miss Fortune gave it to me for being pupil of the week again," Polly told him, stomping off ahead.

Yuck ran after her. "Can I have a bit?"

"No you can't. I'm saving it," Polly said.

She stomped past the bus stop and a dog started barking.

The dog followed Polly, sniffing the Chocolog bar in her hand.

"I promise I'll give you all of MY chocolate," Yuck said.

"That's only because you haven't got any," Polly told him.

The dog's tongue was hanging from its mouth. It was slobbering. It licked Polly's fingers and she jumped. "Uuurgh! What a horrible slobbery dog!"

Yuck laughed.

"It must be hungry," he said.

The dog barked then wagged its tail.

"Go away, you slobbery dog!" Polly yelled.

"It's only being friendly," Yuck told her.

"It's revolting."

The dog was brown and dirty and smelly.

Polly crossed the street and the dog stood at the curb, howling.

Yuck gave it a stroke. "Won't she give you any Chocolog?" he said. "She's mean, isn't she?"

The dog looked cold and hungry. It had a collar and a lead, but there was no sign of its owner.

Yuck looked around. "Are you lost?" he asked it.

"Woof!" the dog barked.

"What's your name?"

Yuck looked at the metal tag on the dog's collar. SCRUFF, he read.

He gave the dog another stroke.

Then, as Yuck crossed the street, the dog crossed the street too. Yuck caught up with Polly, and the dog followed them round the corner and up the road, all the way home.

Yuck and Polly walked up the driveway and the dog followed them to the front door of the house.

"Go away, slobbery dog!" Polly told it.

The dog wagged its tail and barked, "Woof!"

"It's lost," Yuck said. "It needs someone to look after it."

He bent down and the dog licked his face. "Good dog," he said, smiling.

"It's the most horrible dog I've ever seen," Polly said. "It's slobbery and its breath stinks."

"I like it," Yuck told her.

Polly opened the door and went inside.

"Don't worry, Scruff. I'll look after you," Yuck said. He let the dog into the house and it followed him upstairs to his room.

He closed his bedroom door and lay
on the floor to give Scruff a cuddle. Scruff
licked Yuck's face and Yuck laughed.

"You're not horrible at all," Yuck said,
tickling Scruff's tummy. "I think you're the
best dog in the world."

Scruff jumped up and started nosing
around Yuck's carpet.

Yuck watched as the dog sniffed a pair
of his underpants then nuzzled its nose into
a pair of smelly socks.

It licked the wall where Yuck had wiped a bogey then it licked a brown stain on the carpet where he'd spilt some hot chocolate.

"Good dog," Yuck said, giving Scruff a stroke. "Can you do tricks?"

Scruff's tail started wagging.

"Can you sit?"

Scruff sat up straight.

"Shake hands."

The dog held out its right front paw and Yuck shook it.

"Roll over," Yuck said.

Scruff rolled over on Yuck's carpet.

"You are a clever dog," Yuck said.

Just then Mum called from downstairs. "It's dinner time, Yuck!"

"Are you hungry, Scruff?"

"Woof!" the dog barked.

"Let's get you something to eat."

Yuck and Scruff crept downstairs to the kitchen. Mum was taking a tray of sausages out of the oven.

Yuck sat on his chair and Scruff hid under the table at his feet.

Polly and Dad came in and sat down.

"Did you know that Polly was pupil of the week again?" Dad said to Yuck.

"That's because she's a goodie goodie," Yuck said.

"I wish you could be more like your sister, Yuck," Mum said. "Why aren't YOU ever pupil of the week?"

Mum started dishing out sausages, mashed potatoes and Brussels sprouts. "Make sure you eat all your dinner today, Yuck," she said.

Yuck slipped a sausage under the table and Scruff gobbled it. Then Yuck dropped a Brussels sprout and Scruff swallowed it whole. The dog lifted its tail. From under the table came a loud trumpeting **PARP!**

"What was that noise?" Mum asked.

"PHWOAR!" Dad said.

"Yuck, have you let one off?" Polly asked. She was pinching her nose.

"Yuck, that's disgusting!" everyone said.

Yuck was giggling.

He dropped another Brussels sprout for Scruff. The dog ate it under the table then lifted its tail and let out a long squidgy one – **BRRAMP!**

"Yuck, no trouser trumpeting at the table!" Dad said.

Scruff ate another Brussels sprout and let out a big pongy one – **RRRIP!**

Polly jumped off her seat and looked under the table. "It's that dog!" she said.

Mum and Dad bent down to see.

"What on earth is a dog doing in here?" Mum asked.

"It followed us home from school," Polly told her. "It's smelly and horrible. It's a disgusting slobbery dog."

"No he's not. He's a nice dog," Yuck said. "His name's Scruff and he's lost. He needs looking after."

"Well, you can't keep it here," Mum said.

"Please, Mum. Just until I find his owner."

The dog wagged its tail, saliva drooling from its mouth. It slobbered onto Dad's shiny shoe.

Dad leapt up.

"Urgh!" he said, wiping his shoe with a tissue. "That dog's revolting, Yuck! Get it out of here at once!"

"It can go in the garden," Mum said, opening the back door.

Scruff dipped his head sadly and looked up at Yuck with big brown eyes.

"But it's cold outside," Yuck said.

The dog trudged out into the garden, and Yuck ran after it.

"Not you, Yuck," Mum said, closing the door in front of him. "You can play with it in the morning."

"I hope it's gone by then," Polly said, sticking her tongue out at Yuck.

Yuck stormed upstairs to his bedroom.
He opened his window and looked down
at the garden. It was raining outside and it
was starting to get dark. Scruff was sitting
in the middle of the lawn, shivering.

"Poor Scruff," Yuck called down.

Yuck decided that when he was
EMPEROR OF EVERYTHING he'd
have lots of slobbery dogs and they'd ALL
live indoors. They'd eat as many sausages
as they wanted and make music together
parping and barking in a big Doggie Doo
Dah band. Anyone who was mean to
dogs would be taken outside and thrown
into THE SEA OF SLOBBER.

As the rain fell, outside, Scruff began to whine. Then he started to howl.

"Don't worry, Scruff," Yuck called down. "I'll save you."

While Mum, Dad and Polly were in the living room, watching television, Yuck crept downstairs. He sneaked through the kitchen and opened the back door.

Scruff bounded inside and jumped up, licking Yuck's face.

"Good dog," Yuck said, rubbing Scruff dry. He led the dog upstairs to his room.

Yuck lay on his bed and Scruff jumped up beside him, snuggling up in Yuck's duvet.

Scruff scratched himself with his back
leg. Yuck could see lots of little fleas
jumping in the dog's fur.

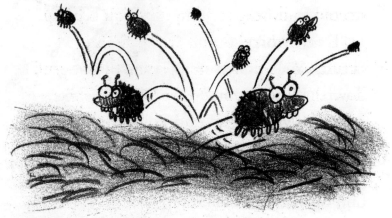

They were hopping up and down.

Rockits! Yuck thought. He had an idea.

He picked the fleas off the dog and put
them in a jar. Then he crept across the
hallway to Polly's bedroom.

He lifted her duvet
and tipped the fleas
into her bed. Then he
dashed out again.

"That'll teach her
to be mean to you,"
Yuck said.

That night, Yuck dreamed he taught
Scruff new tricks. First he taught Scruff
how to jump through a hoop. Then he
taught him how to jump through a hoop
on a motorbike! Scruff was a famous
daredevil dog! The crowds roared as Scruff
flew through the hoop on his motorbike –
juggling sausages!

The next morning, Yuck was woken by a scream from Polly's room.

He jumped out of bed and ran to her door. "What's the matter, Polly?" he asked, giggling.

Polly was standing in her pyjamas, scratching.

"I'm covered in fleas!" she screamed. "They've been biting me all night!"

"I wonder where they came from?" Yuck said.

Scruff ran in, wagging his tail.

"It's that dog! That disgusting dog has given me fleas!" Polly said.

"Go and give Polly a kiss, Scruff," Yuck whispered.

Scruff jumped up to Polly, pinning her against the wall and licking her face.

"Uuurgh!" Polly screamed. She was covered in dog spit. "That's disgusting!"

"Scruff's just being friendly," Yuck said.

"Mum! Come quick!" Polly shouted. "That dog's in my bedroom!"

She pushed Scruff off her.

"Good dog," Yuck said, giving Scruff a stroke.

Mum came into Polly's room. "Yuck, take that dog outside NOW!" she ordered. "Your poor sister is covered in fleas."

While Mum took the sheets off Polly's bed, Scruff took hold of one of Polly's shoes and started chewing.

"Good dog," Yuck whispered. He quickly led Scruff downstairs before anyone could see what Scruff was carrying. "Come on, let's go and play in the garden."

Yuck took Scruff through the kitchen and out the back door.

Outside, the rain had stopped and the sun was out. Mum's washing was hanging on the line.

Scruff dropped Polly's shoe at Yuck's feet. It was wet and sticky with dog spit.

"Good dog," Yuck said. "Now fetch."

Yuck threw the shoe to the end of the garden and Scruff sprinted after it.

The shoe landed in a puddle and Scruff splashed in to get it.

"Good dog," Yuck said. "Now bury it."

The dog carried the shoe to the middle of the garden. It started burrowing with its front paws, digging a hole in the ground.

Yuck watched as Scruff kicked mud all over the clean clothes on the washing line.

Polly came running out of the back door. "Have you seen my shoe, Yuck?" she called.

Polly saw Scruff burying her shoe in the hole. "That dog's got my shoe!" she screamed, running across the garden.

She grabbed the shoe. "It's ruined!" she cried. It was chewed and slobbery.

Then she looked at the washing on the line. Her pink T-shirt was brown!

"My favourite T-shirt's all muddy!" she screamed.

As Polly unpegged it, Scruff grabbed the end of the T-shirt in his teeth.

"Go away, slobbery dog!" Polly said.

"He only wants to play," Yuck told her.

Polly pulled… Scruff pulled… Polly pulled harder…

… **RRRRIIPP!** The T-shirt tore in half and Polly fell in the mud.

Scruff leapt onto her, licking her face, his tongue slobbering up her nose and in her ears, covering her in dog spit.

"Get that slobbery dog off me!" she screamed.

"He's only being friendly," Yuck said.

"I hate you, Yuck!" she screamed. "And I hate that slobbery dog!"

Polly scrambled to her feet and stormed back into the house, clutching her slobbery shoe and her ripped T-shirt.

"Good dog!" Yuck said, giving Scruff a pat.

He crept to the back door and peered inside. The kitchen was empty. He could hear Polly shouting in the bathroom. "It was that slobbery dog!"

She was complaining to Mum and Dad.

"Let's get you dry," Yuck said to Scruff.

Quietly, he led the dog upstairs to Polly's room. "Sit!" he said.

Scruff sat his muddy bottom on Polly's pink rug.

"Roll over!" Yuck said.

The dog rolled over, wiping mud on Polly's rug.

Polly came in.

"Yuck!" she screamed. "What's that slobbery dog doing in here?"

Scruff stood up and shook his fur, spraying mud all over Polly's bedroom.

"Mum! Dad! Quick!" Polly shouted.

Polly ran to find Mum and Dad.

"Good dog," Yuck said to Scruff.

The dog started sniffing. It scratched at Polly's chest of drawers.

Yuck opened the top drawer and saw Polly's Chocolog chocolate bar.

"Is this what you're after?" he asked.

"Woof!" Scruff barked.

The dog jumped up and bit hold of the Chocolog then gobbled it, wrapper and all.

Yuck giggled.

Suddenly, he heard Mum and Dad coming up the stairs.

"Quick, hide!" Yuck said to Scruff. He lifted Polly's duvet and Scruff dived beneath it.

Mum and Dad burst into Polly's room.

"Where's that dog?" Mum asked.

"He's not in here," Yuck told her.

"Polly says you've brought it into the house again."

Polly came in. "It is in here," she said. "I can smell it."

"Yuck, there are muddy paw prints all the way up the stairs," Dad said. "They lead straight to this room."

"Maybe they're Polly's footprints," Yuck replied.

"They're not mine! It's that dog!" Polly shouted. "It's given me fleas, chewed my shoe, ripped my T-shirt, ruined my rug AND made my room all muddy."

Polly saw her drawer open. She checked inside. "And NOW it's eaten my Chocolog!"

Just then, a tail popped out from under her duvet. It was wagging.

Mum pulled the duvet off and saw Scruff on Polly's bedsheet.

Scruff stood up and barked. "Woof!"

In the middle of Polly's bed was a curly lump of dog poo.

"URRRGH!" Mum said.

"That's revolting!" Dad said.

"POO! IT'S POOED IN MY BED!" Polly screamed.

"Yuck, that dog is NEVER to come indoors again!" Mum told him. She grabbed Scruff by the collar and dragged him out of the room and down the stairs.

"But he was only being friendly," Yuck called after her.

Mum dragged Scruff through the kitchen and out into the garden. Then she slammed the back door shut.

Scruff howled at the door.

"He gets lonely out there," Yuck said.

"Tough. Now I want you to clean this mess up," Mum said, pointing to the pawprints on the floor. "After that you can start looking for that dog's owner."

Mum handed Yuck a sponge and a bowl of soapy water.

"But Mum—"

"And make sure you clean Polly's room too!"

While Yuck was scrubbing the stairs, Polly came out of her room wearing her coat.

"You missed a bit," she said, pushing past him.

"Where are you off to?" Yuck asked.

"Mind your own business," Polly said.

She went to the kitchen. "I think I'll take Scruff for a walk, Mum," she said.

"But I thought you didn't like that dog," Mum replied.

"I don't," Polly told her, opening the back door.

"Walkies!" Polly said.

Scruff's tail began wagging.

Polly clipped his lead on.

Scruff tugged on the lead, pulling Polly down the driveway. He dragged her along the pavement and through the town.

"Slow down!" Polly called.

Scruff pulled her through a gate and into the park. Polly let go of the lead. "You're a horrible dog," she said.

Scruff stopped running. He turned and wagged his tail, wanting to play.

"It's time to get rid of you for good."

Polly picked up a stick and threw it as far as she could, over the swings to the bushes.

"Fetch," she said.

Scruff set off with the lead trailing behind him.

As he raced to find the stick, Polly ran to a tree. She climbed up it and hid among the branches. Then she looked across the park, sniggering as Scruff came back to find her.

The dog was carrying the stick in its mouth. It stood, looking for her. But it couldn't find her.

Polly watched as Scruff ran to the swings then back to the bushes.

The dog was darting from bush to bush, looking everywhere for her. It began whining and howling.

"What a stupid slobbery dog," Polly muttered to herself. She was smiling.

She watched as Scruff ran off through the park to look for her. When he was out of sight, she climbed down the tree. "Good riddance," she said.

She walked out of the gates and laughed all the way home.

When she arrived, Yuck was in the kitchen with Mum. He'd finished his cleaning.

"Mum, can I go and play with Scruff now?" he asked.

"Scruff's gone," Polly said.

Yuck ran to the back door and looked out. "What do you mean, gone?"

"I took him to the park and he ran off," Polly said.

"Maybe he went back to his owner," Mum said.

"Maybe he didn't like you, Yuck," Polly said. She stuck her tongue out.

"What have you done to him?" Yuck asked, racing out of the door.

"Yuck, where are you going?" Mum called.

"I'm going to find Scruff!"

Yuck raced down the driveway and along the road. "Here Scruff! Here doggie!" he called.

He ran into the town. "Here Scruff!"

He ran to the park. "Scruff, where are you? Here Scruff!"

Yuck couldn't find the dog anywhere.

He ran past the swings, calling. "Scruff!"

He ran around the pond. "Scruff!"

Then he ran past an old lady. "Scruff!"

The old lady was pinning a piece of paper to a tree. "What did you say?" she asked.

Yuck stopped. "I was calling my dog."

He looked at the piece of paper on the tree. On it was a picture of Scruff!

Above the picture it said: LOST DOG. Below the picture it said: REWARD.

"Did I hear you say Scruff?" the old lady asked.

"Yes," Yuck said. "I've been looking after him, but my sister took him for a walk and—"

"Woof!" Yuck heard a bark.

He turned and saw Scruff sprinting towards him from the bushes.

The dog ran over, jumped up and licked Yuck's face.

"There's a good dog," Yuck said.

Then Scruff jumped up to the old lady and licked her face too.

"Oh, Scruff, I've been looking for you everywhere," the old lady said.

"Woof!" Scruff barked. His tail was wagging. He was so excited.

He rolled over, then sat up, then shook Yuck's hand.

"He's a very clever dog," Yuck said.

Scruff did a big poo and the old lady scooped it up and popped it in a plastic bag.

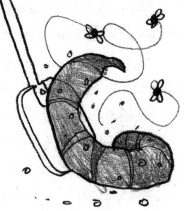

"Please could you hold this for me?" she asked, handing the bag to Yuck.

Yuck held the bag of poo while the lady fumbled in her coat pocket and took out her purse.

"Well, here you are," she said, handing Yuck a ten-pound note.

"Is that for me?" Yuck asked.

"It's your reward," the old lady said.

Yuck looked at the money. Rockits! he thought.

Then he looked at Scruff.

"Can I come and visit him?" Yuck asked.

The old lady handed Yuck a piece of paper with her telephone number on it. "Make sure you tell your Mum, and you can take him for walks in the park whenever you like."

Yuck smiled. He gave Scruff a big hug and the dog licked his face. "I'll see you soon, Scruff," Yuck said.

Yuck waved as the old lady led Scruff across the park. Then he walked to the gate, happy that Scruff was going to his proper home.

Yuck turned and looked back.
"Hang on, you
forgot something,"
he called, holding up
the bag of dog poo.

But the old lady
had gone.

Yuck tucked the
bag in his pocket and headed home.

On the way back, he stopped at Candy
Joe's sweet shop to spend his reward money.

"Please can I have ten pounds' worth of
Chocolog chocolate bars?" he asked.

Candy Joe gave Yuck a bumper box full
of Chocologs.

"Thank you," Yuck
said, lifting the box
off the counter.

All the way home
he scoffed the
Chocologs, undoing their gold wrappers
and eating them one after the other.

They were delicious!

"Did you find the dog?" Mum asked when Yuck got back.

"Yes. And I found his owner, too," Yuck told her. "Scruff's gone home now."

"Good," Polly said.

Yucked walked through the kitchen carrying the box of Chocologs.

"Hang on, where did you get those?" Polly asked.

"They were a reward," he said, unwrapping a Chocolog and scoffing it in front of her.

"A reward?"

"For looking after Scruff."

"That's not fair," Polly said. "Where's MY reward?"

"You didn't look after Scruff, Polly. You said he was a horrible dog."

Yuck ran to his room.

Polly banged on his door. "I want a Chocolog!" she said. "That dog ate mine!"

Yuck felt in his pocket. Inside was the bag with the lump of dog poo. He took the poo out then wrapped it in a gold Chocolog wrapper.

Mum opened the door. "Yuck, please will you share your chocolate with Polly?"

"Oh, all right," Yuck said.

He handed Polly the dog poo wrapped in the gold wrapper.

She tore the wrapper off and bit into it. Her mouth squelched.

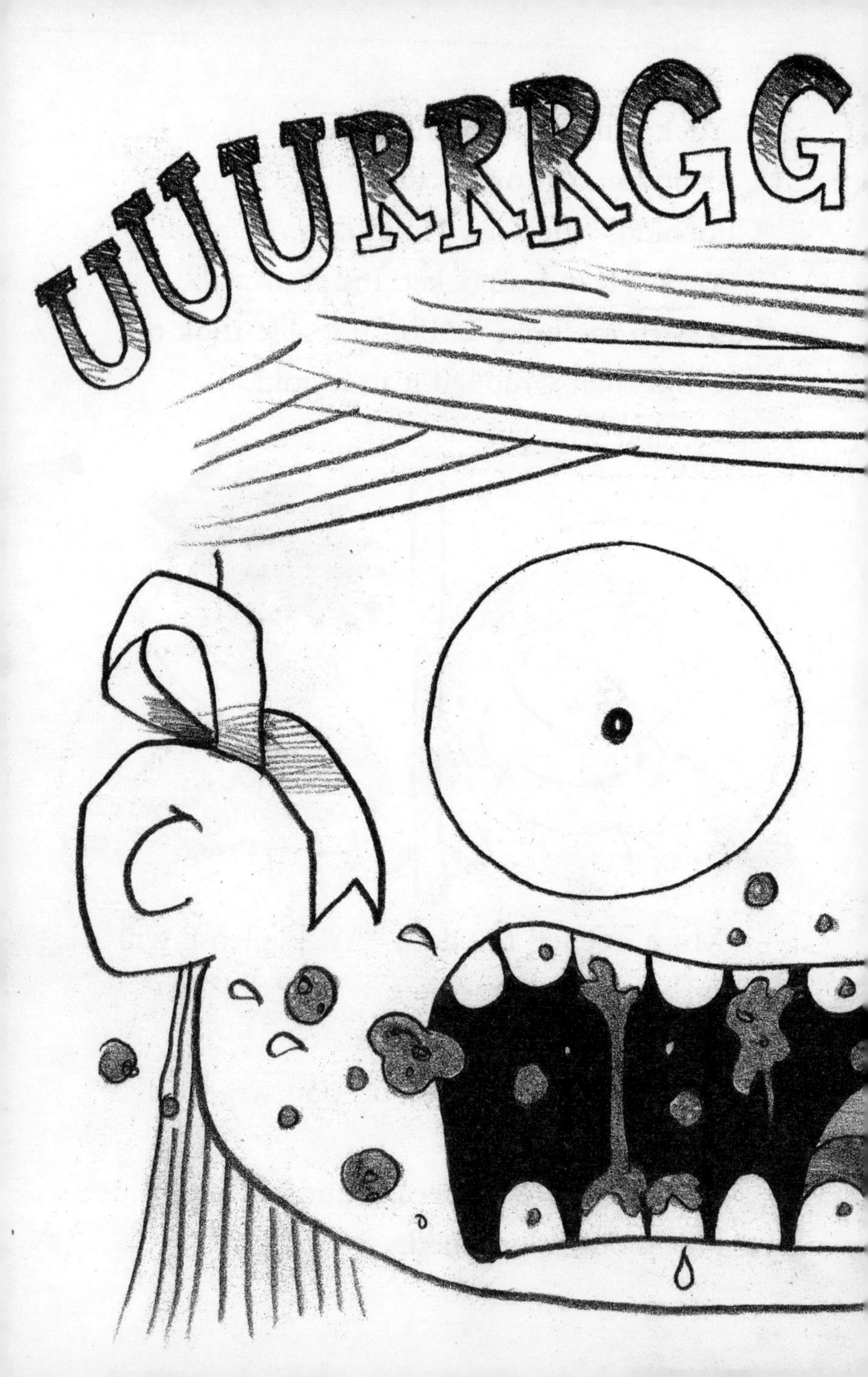
UUURRRGG

The dog poo melted on her tongue and stuck between her teeth.

Mum looked at her.

Polly's face was turning green.

"What's the matter, Polly?" Mum asked.

"This isn't chocolate!" Polly cried.

Yuck was sitting on his bed, giggling.

"It's your reward," he said. "It's a present from Scruff."

Become a member of Yuck's fanclub at:

WWW.YUCKWEB.COM

Find Matt and Dave's rotten jokes, gross games and disgusting downloads, as well as crazy competitions AND the first word on Yuck's new adventures.

Be warned: it's really Yucky!